MW01174448

Training Pickles

Story by Carmel Reilly

Illustrations by Pat Reynolds

Contents

Chapter 1

Pickles Does Well

"Sit, Pickles," said Nina,
and she pulled at his lead.

Pickles looked up at Nina and barked.

"No, Pickles," said Nina. "Sit down."
She pulled on the lead again.

This time, Pickles sat down.
"Good dog!" said Nina,
and she gave him a puppy treat.

"Pickles is doing well," said the trainer.
"Remember to keep up the training at home.
And only give him puppy treats
when he has done the right thing."

"I will," said Nina.

Chapter 2

A Game of Chasey

That afternoon,
Nina's friend, Eddie from next door,
came over.

Pickles barked when he saw Eddie.

"Pickles likes me," said Eddie, laughing.

Eddie ran quickly up and down the garden.
Pickles followed him, barking.

Eddie and Pickles ran back to Nina.

"I have been training Pickles," said Nina.
"I'll show you what he can do now.
Watch this!"

Nina looked at Pickles.
"Sit, Pickles," she said.

But Pickles didn't hear her.
He was jumping and barking,
and looking up at Eddie.

"Pickles!" called Nina.

Pickles looked around.
Nina took a puppy treat out of her pocket
and held it up.

"Sit, Pickles," she said.

But the treat slipped from Nina's hand
and dropped onto the grass.

"Oh, no!" cried Nina.
She grabbed for the treat,
but it was too late.
Pickles already had it in his mouth.

Chapter 3

Clever Dog

Pickles looked up at Nina and barked.

"I think he wants another one," said Eddie, laughing.

"This isn't funny, Eddie," said Nina. "Look, Pickles won't sit down now. How will I get him to do what I want when you are laughing at him?"

"What did you do at puppy training school?"
asked Eddie.

"When something didn't work,
the trainer told us to try again," she said.

Nina held up another treat for Pickles to see and said, "Sit, Pickles."

Pickles looked at the treat
and turned his head to one side.
Then he looked up at Nina.

"S. . . i. . . t," Nina said again, slowly.

And Pickles sat down.

Nina gave Pickles the treat and a big pat.
"You are a clever dog, Pickles," she said.

"He's going to be trained in no time at all,"
said Eddie.